THOMAS & FRIENDS™

The Lost Puff

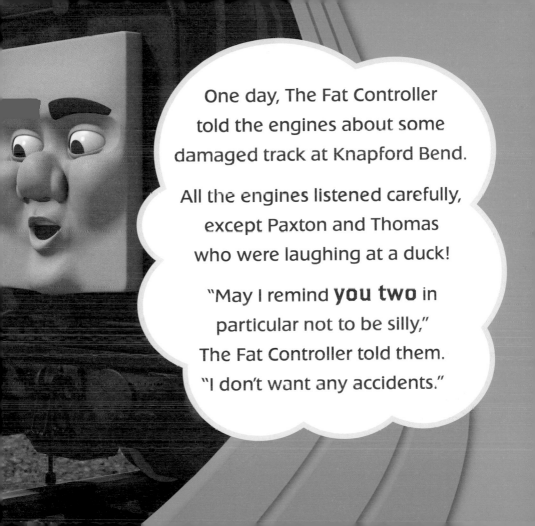

One day, The Fat Controller told the engines about some damaged track at Knapford Bend.

All the engines listened carefully, except Paxton and Thomas who were laughing at a duck!

"May I remind **you two** in particular not to be silly," The Fat Controller told them. "I don't want any accidents."

Later, Paxton arrived at the broken track. As he rolled over it, it rattled his radiator, making him laugh.

"That was fun!" he grinned. And when Thomas appeared, Paxton got him to try it too.

"Woo-hooooo," Thomas giggled, as he bounced along.

"Get a good run up and go really fast over it," Paxton suggested.

So Thomas raced backwards around the corner and …

… **bashed** into Toby, who was filling up at the water tower!

Water **sploshed** all over Thomas, which put out his firebox.

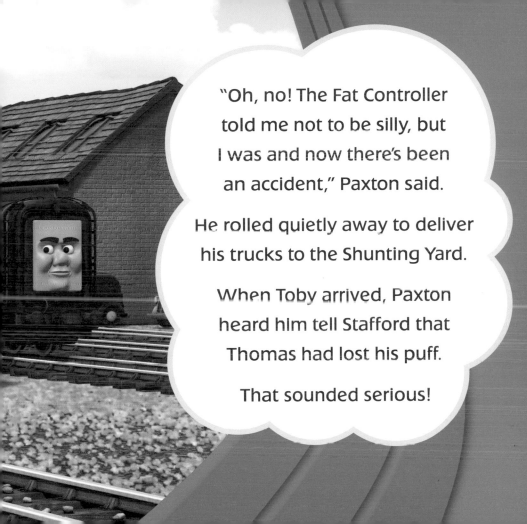

"Oh, no! The Fat Controller told me not to be silly, but I was and now there's been an accident," Paxton said.

He rolled quietly away to deliver his trucks to the Shunting Yard.

When Toby arrived, Paxton heard him tell Stafford that Thomas had lost his puff.

That sounded serious!

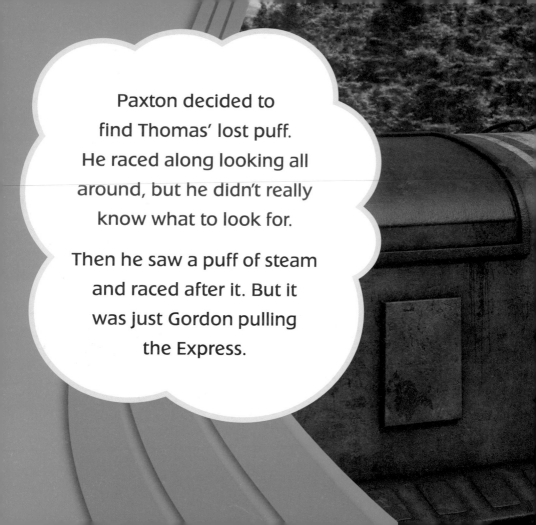

Paxton decided to find Thomas' lost puff. He raced along looking all around, but he didn't really know what to look for.

Then he saw a puff of steam and raced after it. But it was just Gordon pulling the Express.

Next, Paxton spotted a **fluffy** cloud in the sky.

"That must be Thomas' missing puff!" he said as he hurried towards it.

Paxton followed the cloud all the way to Ulfstead Castle, where he met Stephen.

"Hello, Paxton," said Stephen. "What are you doing here?"

"Thomas lost his puff and I thought that might be it," Paxton told him.

"Up there? That's just a cloud," Stephen replied.

Paxton felt rather silly. He sped away as fast as his wheels could carry him.

Paxton realised he didn't know about steam engines' puff because he's a diesel engine.

But he knew someone who did know about steam engines: Victor, who repaired them!

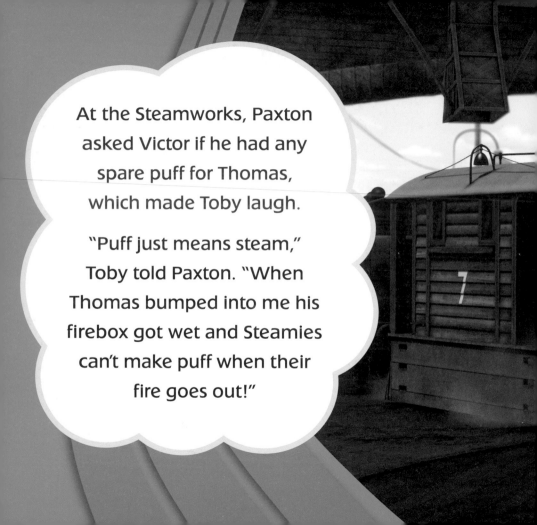

At the Steamworks, Paxton asked Victor if he had any spare puff for Thomas, which made Toby laugh.

"Puff just means steam," Toby told Paxton. "When Thomas bumped into me his firebox got wet and Steamies can't make puff when their fire goes out!"

Yet again Paxton felt silly, but he cheered up when he realised that Thomas would be fine when his firebox dried out.

As Paxton sped back to the water tower, he heard a *peep* and Thomas puffed around the corner.

"You're OK!" Paxton said.

"Yes, I found my puff!" Thomas joked.

"At least I *learned* something today," Paxton smiled.

"That puff means steam?" asked Thomas.

"Yes, but also that when The Fat Controller tells me not to be silly, I shouldn't be silly!" smiled Paxton. And Thomas agreed!

PEEP! PEEP!

The End